To Sleep with the Angels

By H. Elizabeth Collins

Illustrations by Judy Kuusisto

ILLUMINATION ARTS
PUBLISHING COMPANY, INC.
BELLEVUE, WASHINGTON

ILLUMINATION
Arts

PUBLISHING COMPANY, INC.

P. O. Box 1865, Bellevue, WA 98009
Tel: 425-644-7185 ★ 888-210-8216 (orders only) ★ Fax: 426-644-9274
liteinfo@illumin.com ★ www.illumin.com

Library of Congress Cataloging-in-Publication Data

Collins, H. Elizabeth, 1972-
    To sleep with the angels / words by H. Elizabeth Collins ; illustrations
    by Judy Kuusisto
          p. cm.
    Summary: A young child is guided and protected through the night by a
special angel.
    ISBN 0-935699-16-3
    [1. Angels—Fiction.]   I. Kuusisto, Judy, 1946-   ill.   II. Title.
PZ7.C6964To   1999
[Fic]—dc21
                                   98-43247
                                      CIP
                                      AC

Published in the United States of America
Printed by Star Standard Industries in Singapore

Book Designer:
Molly Murrah, Murrah & Company, Kirkland, WA

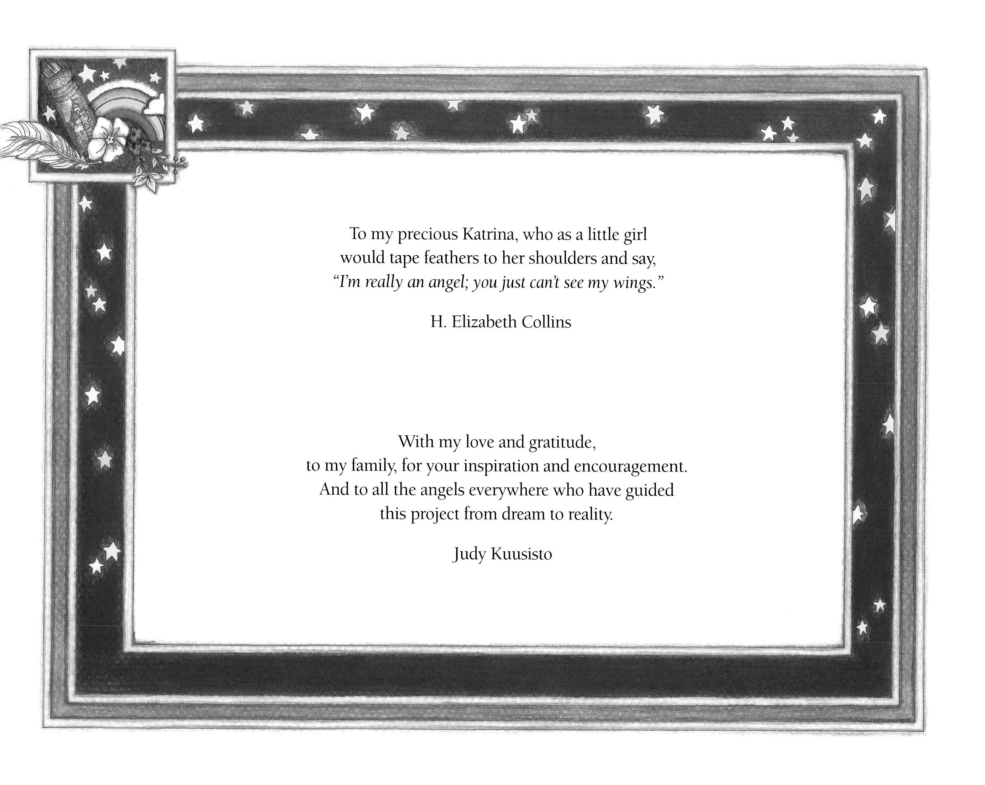

To my precious Katrina, who as a little girl
would tape feathers to her shoulders and say,
"I'm really an angel; you just can't see my wings."

H. Elizabeth Collins

With my love and gratitude,
to my family, for your inspiration and encouragement.
And to all the angels everywhere who have guided
this project from dream to reality.

Judy Kuusisto

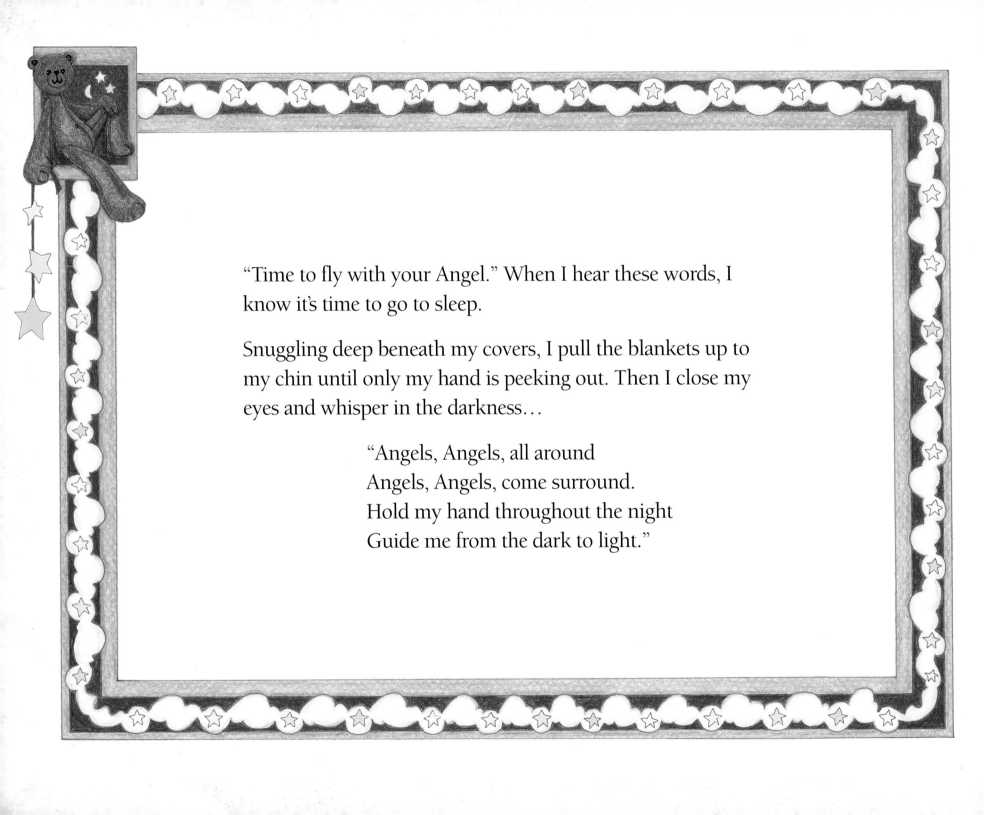

"Time to fly with your Angel." When I hear these words, I know it's time to go to sleep.

Snuggling deep beneath my covers, I pull the blankets up to my chin until only my hand is peeking out. Then I close my eyes and whisper in the darkness…

"Angels, Angels, all around
Angels, Angels, come surround.
Hold my hand throughout the night
Guide me from the dark to light."

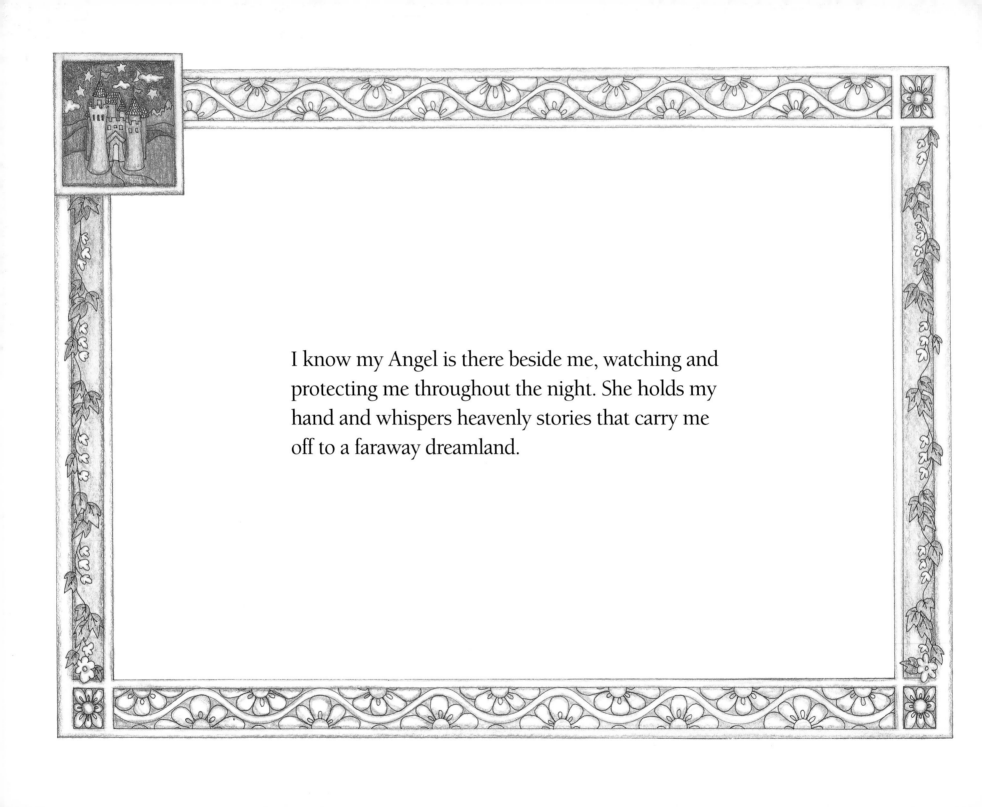

I know my Angel is there beside me, watching and protecting me throughout the night. She holds my hand and whispers heavenly stories that carry me off to a faraway dreamland.

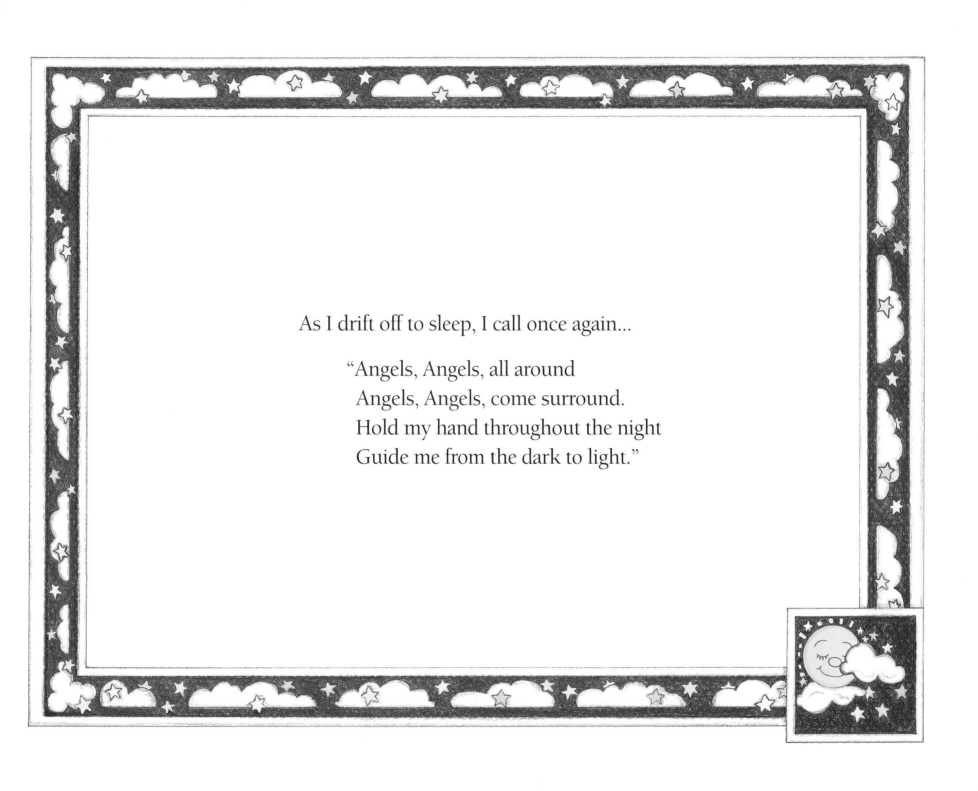

As I drift off to sleep, I call once again...

"Angels, Angels, all around
    Angels, Angels, come surround.
    Hold my hand throughout the night
    Guide me from the dark to light."

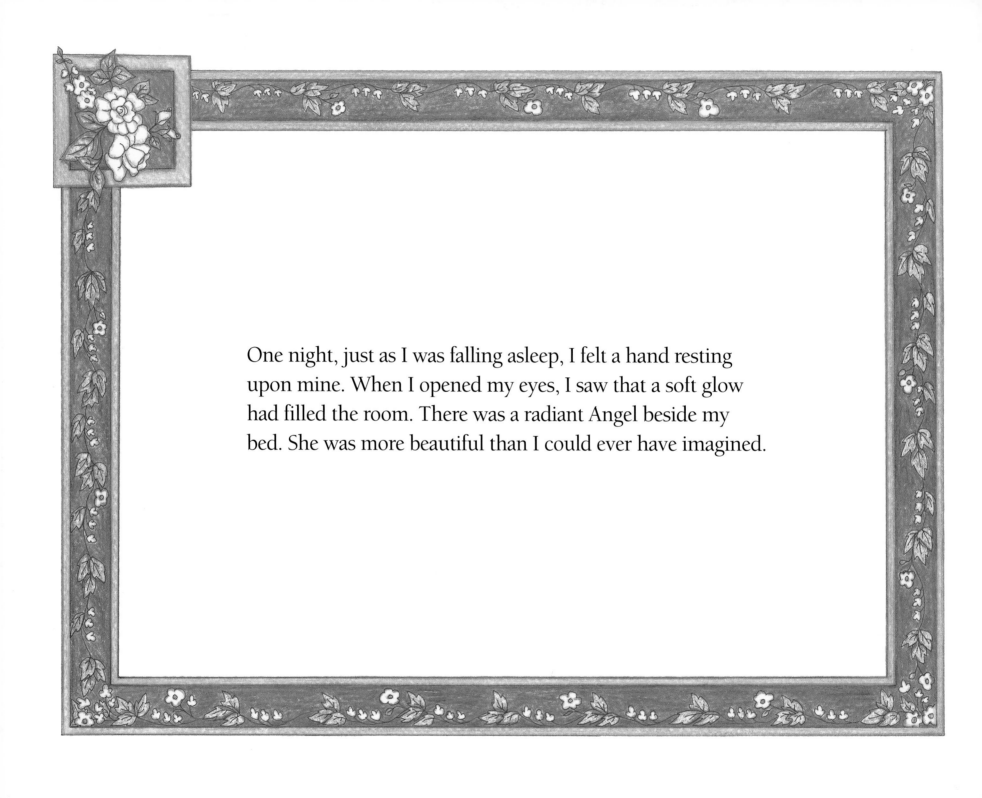

One night, just as I was falling asleep, I felt a hand resting upon mine. When I opened my eyes, I saw that a soft glow had filled the room. There was a radiant Angel beside my bed. She was more beautiful than I could ever have imagined.

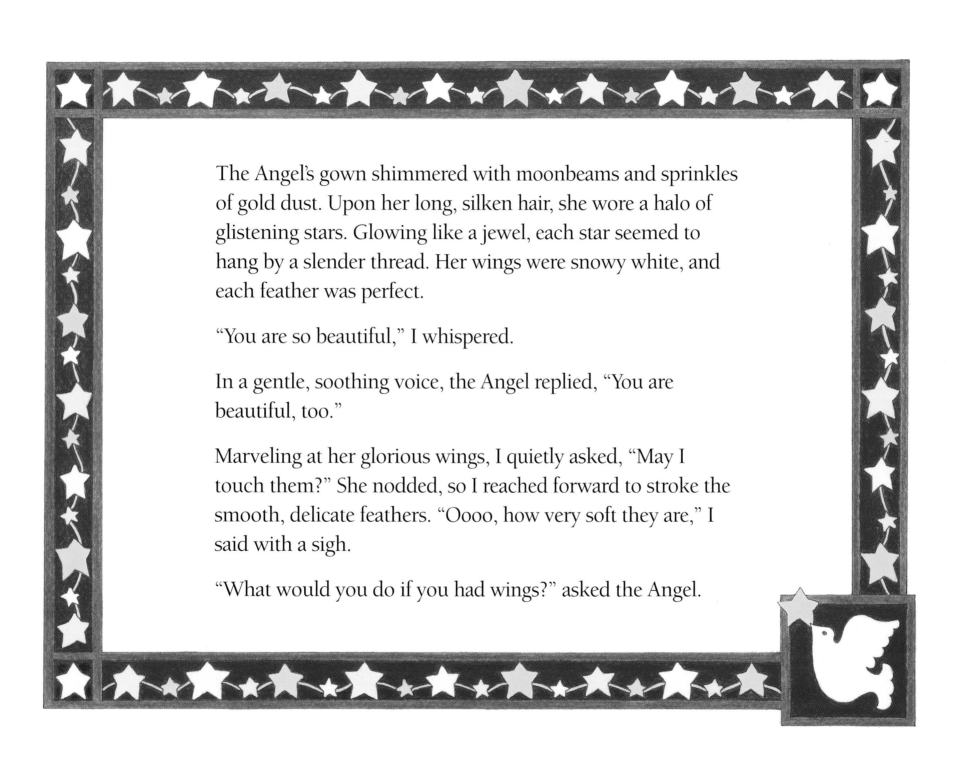

The Angel's gown shimmered with moonbeams and sprinkles of gold dust. Upon her long, silken hair, she wore a halo of glistening stars. Glowing like a jewel, each star seemed to hang by a slender thread. Her wings were snowy white, and each feather was perfect.

"You are so beautiful," I whispered.

In a gentle, soothing voice, the Angel replied, "You are beautiful, too."

Marveling at her glorious wings, I quietly asked, "May I touch them?" She nodded, so I reached forward to stroke the smooth, delicate feathers. "Oooo, how very soft they are," I said with a sigh.

"What would you do if you had wings?" asked the Angel.

"If I had wings, I would soar high into the sky
and make a necklace out of stars!"

"I would dance among the clouds,
playing with all the fluffy cloud animals."

"I would fly to the top of a rainbow and slide all the way down."

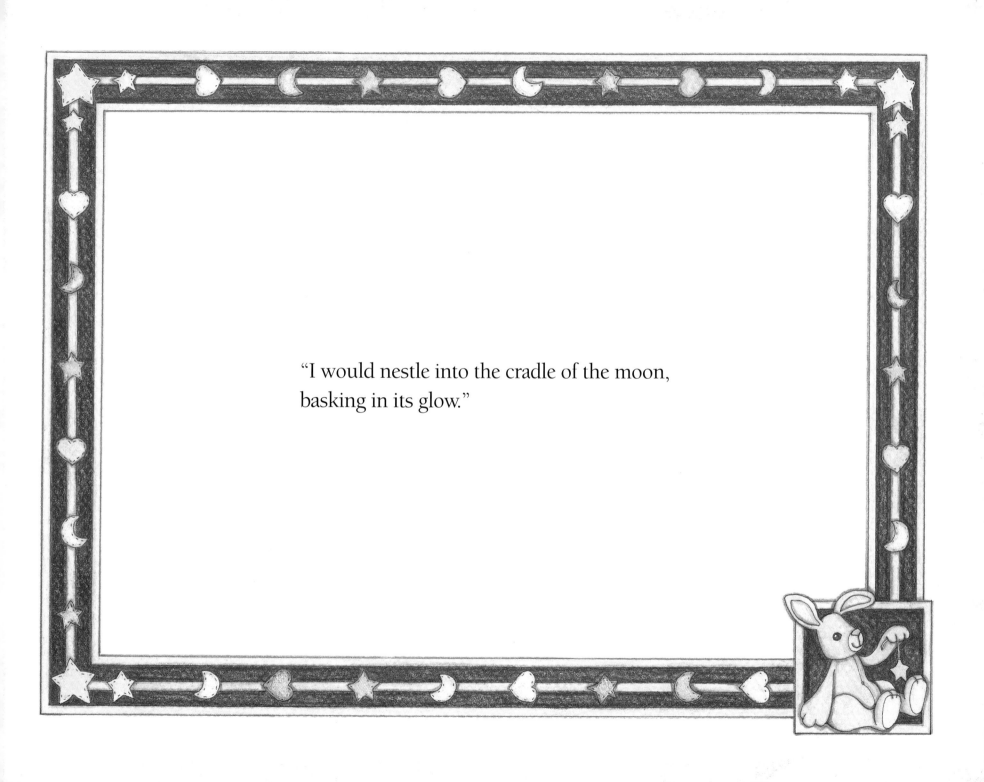

"I would nestle into the cradle of the moon,
basking in its glow."

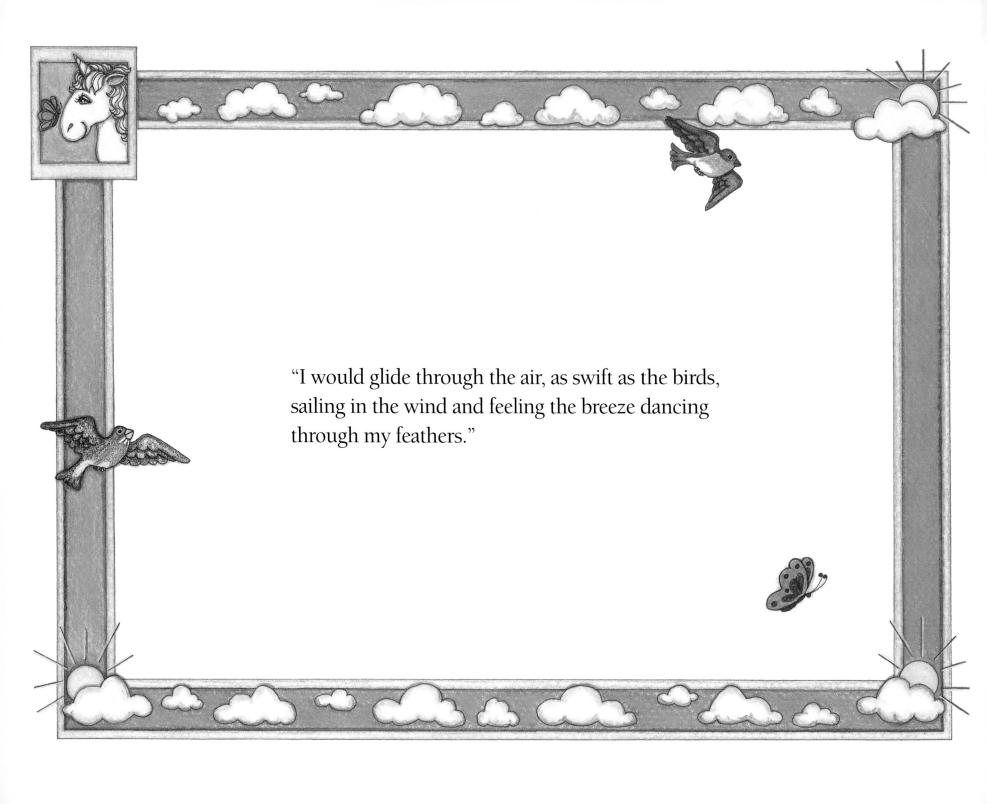

"I would glide through the air, as swift as the birds, sailing in the wind and feeling the breeze dancing through my feathers."

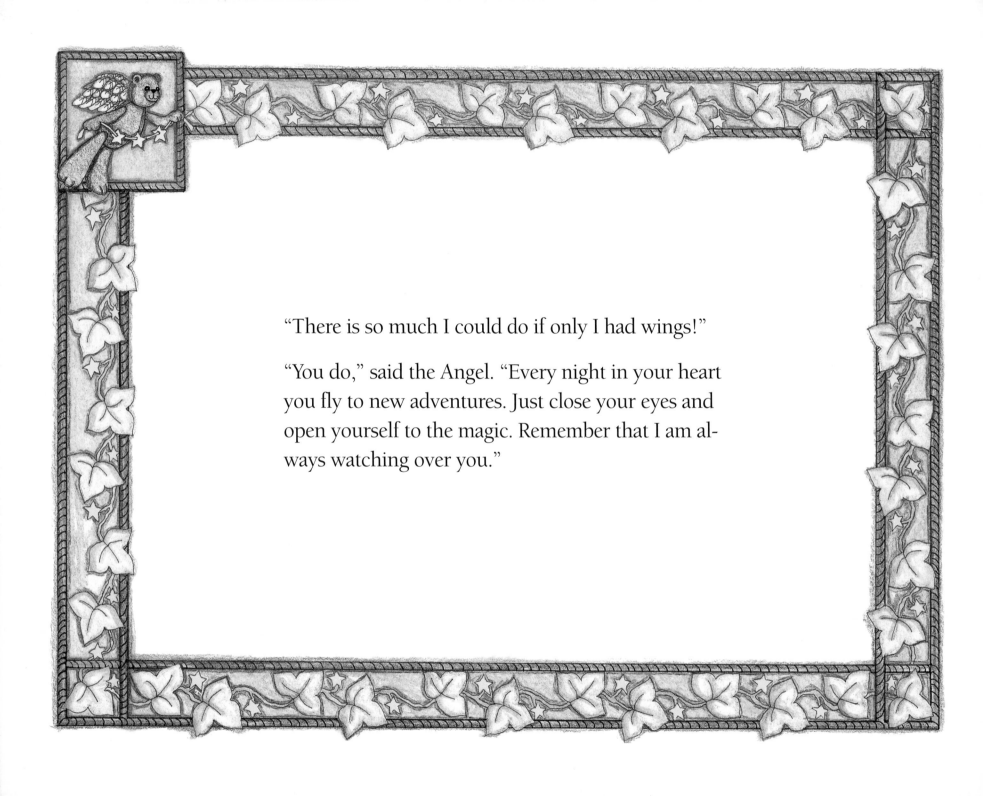

"There is so much I could do if only I had wings!"

"You do," said the Angel. "Every night in your heart you fly to new adventures. Just close your eyes and open yourself to the magic. Remember that I am always watching over you."

I awoke wondering if my Angel's visit had been just a dream. Then I saw something at the foot of my bed. I sat up to take a closer look and found a perfect snowy-white feather that was as soft as velvet.

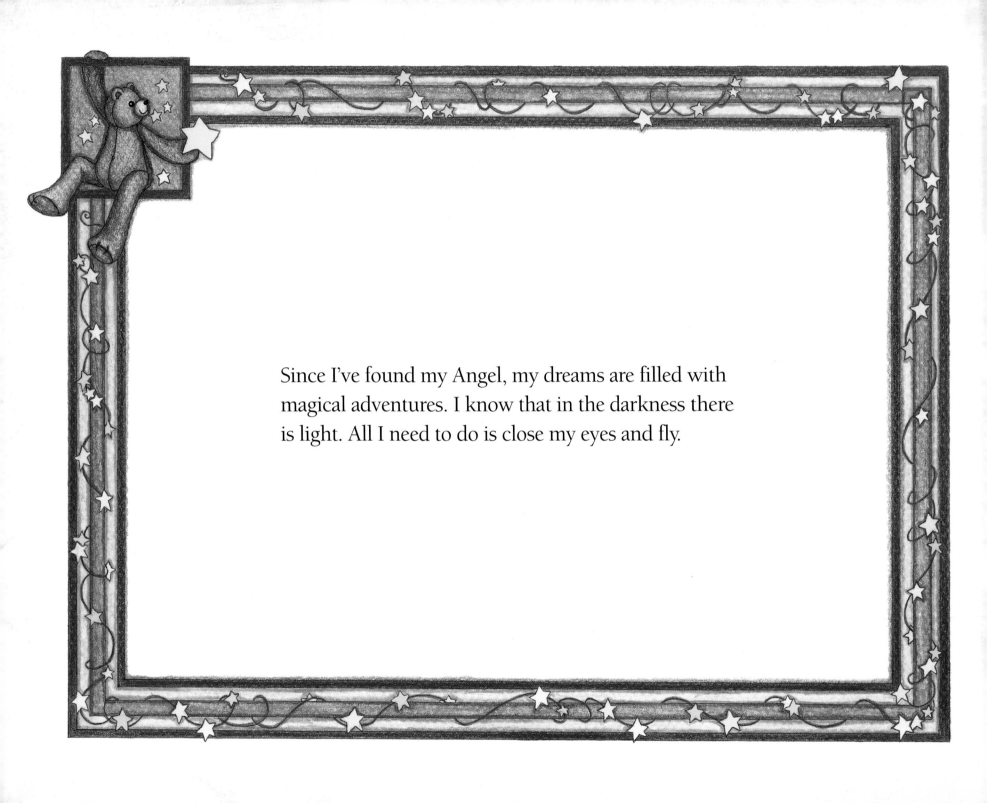

Since I've found my Angel, my dreams are filled with magical adventures. I know that in the darkness there is light. All I need to do is close my eyes and fly.

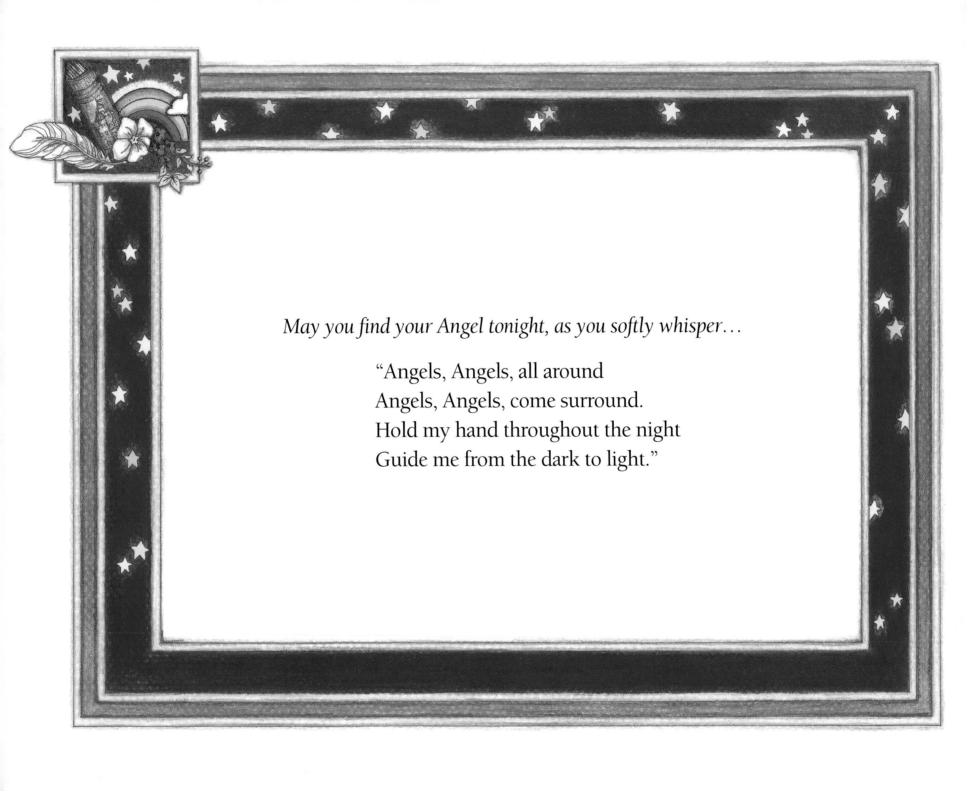

May you find your Angel tonight, as you softly whisper…

"Angels, Angels, all around
Angels, Angels, come surround.
Hold my hand throughout the night
Guide me from the dark to light."

H. Elizabeth Collins

Photo © Marcus Schoenherr

A native Minnesotan, H. Elizabeth Collins now lives in San Diego, California. "With this book, I am beginning a new life," she says. "I've just been married and hope to start a family and adopt a dog!" Her passions include writing, children, and collecting angels. Holding a B.A. in Cultural Anthropology and an M.A. in Human Development, Elizabeth is continuing her education in holistic health therapies while volunteering as a hospice worker.

Judy Kuusisto

Photo © Connie Meyers

A graduate of the University of Minnesota, Judy Kuusisto is a multi-talented artist. She has been a weaver, sculptor, doll maker, commercial artist, giftware designer, and art teacher. She lives with her husband on a lake in Northern Minnesota where loon calls are heard frequently and wildlife is abundant. Though her three children are grown, Judy's household includes a variety of dogs, cats, ferrets, and even hedgehogs – not to mention the out-doors animals.

THE BONSAI BEAR
By Bernard Libster, illust. by Aries Cheung $15.95, 0-935699-15-5

Issa, a Japanese bonsai master, and his wife are given an orphan bear cub who quickly wins their hearts. Issa uses bonsai techniques to keep him from growing, but the playful bear dreams of being wild and free. Ages 4 to adult.

DRAGON
Written and illustrated by Jody Bergsma $15.95, 0-935699-17-1

Born on the same day, a gentle prince and a firebreathing dragon share a prophetic destiny before the Prince can become King. Ages 5 to adult.

SKY CASTLE
By Sandra Hanken, illust. by Jody Bergsma $15.95, 0-935699-14-7

Selected as a "Children's Choice for 1999" by Children's Book Council

High above the clouds, three charming fairies help us create a majestic castle for all the worlds creatures. This colorful Celtic tale, alive with winged dragons and teddy bears, inspires children of all ages to believe in the power of dreams. Ages 3 to adult.

DREAMBIRDS
By David Ogden, illust. by Jody Bergsma $16.95, 0-935699-090

1998 Visionary Award for Best Children's Book–Coalition of Visionary Retailers

The magical story of a Native American boy's search for the gift of the illusive dreambird. Spectacular illustrations of Northwest wildlife "exceed the highest standards for the genre." – Birdwatchers Digest. Ages 5 to adult.

THE RIGHT TOUCH
A Read-Aloud Story to Help Prevent Child Sexual Abuse
By Sandy Kleven, LCSW, illust. by Jody Bergsma $15.95, 0-935699-10-4

Winner – 1999 Benjamin Franklin Award

In The Right Touch, young Jimmy's mother gently explains how he can protect himself from improper touching. Selected as Outstanding by the Parents Council®, this book is suitable for children as young as age 3.

ALL I SEE IS PART OF ME
By Chara M. Curtis, illust. by Cynthia Aldrich $15.95, 0-935699-07-4

Winner – 1996 Award of Excellence from Body Mind Spirit Magazine

This inspirational classic appeals to all ages, as a child discovers his common link with the Universe. Inspired by Sister Star, he feels the light within his heart and then finds that same light in all others. Readers' hearts are deeply touched. Ages 2 to adult.

FUN IS A FEELING
By Chara M. Curtis, illust. by Cynthia Aldrich $15.95, 0-935699-13-9

Refreshing rhymes and inspiring illustrations encourage readers to discover the fun hidden in all of life's experiences. "Fun isn't something or somewhere or who. It's a feeling of joy that lives inside of you." Ages 3 to adult.

HOW FAR TO HEAVEN?
By Chara M. Curtis, illust. by Alfred Currier $15.95, 0-935699-06-6

Nanna and her granddaughter explore the wonders of nature to discover how close heaven really is. A magnificently illustrated favorite with nature-lovers and those who have lost a loved one. Ages 4 to adult.

CORNELIUS AND THE DOG STAR
By Diana Spyropulos, illust. by Ray Williams $15.95, 0-935699-08-2

Winner – 1996 Award of Excellence from Body Mind Spirit Magazine

After grouchy old Cornelius Basset-Hound takes his last breath, he is swept directly to the gates of Dog Heaven. His amazing adventure begins when Saint Bernard says he must learn about love, generosity, and playfulness. Ages 4 to adult.

ILLUMINATION Arts
PUBLISHING COMPANY
PO. Box 1865, Bellevue, WA 98009
Tel: 425-644-7185 ★ Fax: 425-644-9274
888-210-8216
literinfo@illumin.com ★ http://www.illumin.com

Direct U.S. orders: Add $2.00 for postage; each additional book, add $1.00.
Washington residents, add 8.6% state sales tax.